For more information on about discounts for bulk purchases, please contact: sbmoorepublishing@gmail.com

Cover Designed by Sam Johnson

ISBN: 978-1-917121-90-3 (Trade Paperback)

ISBN: 978-1-917121-91-0 (eBook)

THE VERY BEST
CLASSIC SHORT STORIES

VOLUME ONE

CONTENTS

A PAIR OF
SILK STOCKINGS

Kate Chopin

Little Mrs. Sommers one day found herself the unexpected possessor of fifteen dollars. It seemed to her a very large amount of money, and the way in which it stuffed and bulged her worn old porte-monnaie gave her a feeling of importance such as she had not enjoyed for years.

The question of investment was one that occupied her greatly. For a day or two she walked about apparently in a dreamy state, but really absorbed in speculation and calculation. She did not wish to act hastily, to do anything she might afterward regret. But it was during the still hours of the night when she lay awake revolving plans in her mind that she seemed to see her way clearly toward a proper and judicious use of the money.

A dollar or two should be added to the price usually paid for Janie's shoes, which would insure their lasting an appreciable time longer than they usually did. She would buy so and so many yards of percale for new shirt waists for the boys and Janie and Mag. She had intended to make the old ones do by skilful patching. Mag should have another gown. She had seen some beautiful patterns, veritable bargains in the shop windows. And still there would be left enough for new stockings—two pairs apiece—and what darning that would save for a while! She would get caps for the boys and sailor-hats for the girls. The vision of her little brood looking fresh and dainty and new for once in their lives excited her and made her restless and wakeful with anticipation.

The neighbors sometimes talked of certain "better days" that little Mrs. Sommers had known before she had ever thought of being Mrs. Sommers. She herself indulged in no such morbid retrospection. She had no time—no second of time to devote to the past. The needs of the present absorbed her every faculty. A vision of the future like some dim, gaunt monster sometimes appalled her, but luckily to-morrow never comes.

Mrs. Sommers was one who knew the value of bargains; who could stand for hours making her way inch by inch toward the desired object that was selling below cost. She could elbow her way if need be; she had learned to clutch a piece of goods and hold it and stick to it with persistence and determination till her turn came to be served, no matter when it came.

But that day she was a little faint and tired. She had swallowed a light luncheon—no! when she came to think of it, between getting the children fed and the place righted, and preparing herself for the shopping bout, she had actually forgotten to eat any luncheon at all!

She sat herself upon a revolving stool before a counter that was comparatively deserted, trying to gather strength and courage to charge through an eager multitude that was besieging breastworks of shirting and figured lawn. An all-gone limp feeling had come over her and she rested her hand aimlessly upon the counter. She wore no gloves. By degrees she grew aware that her hand had encountered something very soothing, very pleasant to touch. She looked down to see that her hand lay upon a pile of silk stockings. A placard near by announced that they had been reduced in price from two dollars and fifty cents to one dollar and ninety-eight cents; and a young girl who stood behind the counter asked her if she wished to examine their line of silk hosiery. She smiled, just as if she had been asked to inspect a tiara of diamonds with the ultimate view of purchasing it. But she went on feeling the soft, sheeny luxurious things—with both hands now, holding them up to see them glisten, and to feel them glide serpent-like through her fingers.

Two hectic blotches came suddenly into her pale cheeks. She looked up at the girl.

"Do you think there are any eights-and-a-half among these?"

There were any number of eights-and-a-half. In fact,

there were more of that size than any other. Here was a light-blue pair; there were some lavender, some all black and various shades of tan and gray. Mrs. Sommers selected a black pair and looked at them very long and closely. She pretended to be examining their texture, which the clerk assured her was excellent.

"A dollar and ninety-eight cents," she mused aloud. "Well, I'll take this pair." She handed the girl a five-dollar bill and waited for her change and for her parcel. What a very small parcel it was! It seemed lost in the depths of her shabby old shopping-bag.

Mrs. Sommers after that did not move in the direction of the bargain counter. She took the elevator, which carried her to an upper floor into the region of the ladies' waiting-rooms. Here, in a retired corner, she exchanged her cotton stockings for the new silk ones which she had just bought. She was not going through any acute mental process or reasoning with herself, nor was she striving to explain to her satisfaction the motive of her action. She was not thinking at all. She seemed for the time to be taking a rest from that laborious and fatiguing function and to have abandoned herself to some mechanical impulse that directed her actions and freed her of responsibility.

How good was the touch of the raw silk to her flesh!

She felt like lying back in the cushioned chair and reveling for a while in the luxury of it. She did for a little while. Then she replaced her shoes, rolled the cotton stockings together and thrust them into her bag. After doing this she crossed straight over to the shoe department and took her seat to be fitted.

She was fastidious. The clerk could not make her out; he could not reconcile her shoes with her stockings, and she was not too easily pleased. She held back her skirts and turned her feet one way and her head another way as she glanced down at the polished, pointed-tipped boots. Her foot and ankle looked very pretty. She could not realize that they belonged to her and were a part of herself. She wanted an excellent and stylish fit, she told the young fellow who served her, and she did not mind the difference of a dollar or two more in the price so long as she got what she desired.

It was a long time since Mrs. Sommers had been fitted with gloves. On rare occasions when she had bought a pair they were always "bargains," so cheap that it would have been preposterous and unreasonable to have expected them to be fitted to the hand.

Now she rested her elbow on the cushion of the glove counter, and a pretty, pleasant young creature, delicate and deft of touch, drew a long-wristed "kid" over Mrs.

Sommers's hand. She smoothed it down over the wrist and buttoned it neatly, and both lost themselves for a second or two in admiring contemplation of the little symmetrical gloved hand. But there were other places where money might be spent.

There were books and magazines piled up in the window of a stall a few paces down the street. Mrs. Sommers bought two high-priced magazines such as she had been accustomed to read in the days when she had been accustomed to other pleasant things. She carried them without wrapping. As well as she could she lifted her skirts at the crossings. Her stockings and boots and well fitting gloves had worked marvels in her bearing—had given her a feeling of assurance, a sense of belonging to the well-dressed multitude.

She was very hungry. Another time she would have stilled the cravings for food until reaching her own home, where she would have brewed herself a cup of tea and taken a snack of anything that was available. But the impulse that was guiding her would not suffer her to entertain any such thought.

There was a restaurant at the corner. She had never entered its doors; from the outside she had sometimes caught glimpses of spotless damask and shining crystal, and soft-stepping waiters serving people of fashion.

When she entered her appearance created no surprise, no consternation, as she had half feared it might. She seated herself at a small table alone, and an attentive waiter at once approached to take her order. She did not want a profusion; she craved a nice and tasty bite—a half dozen blue-points, a plump chop with cress, a something sweet—a crème-frappée, for instance; a glass of Rhine wine, and after all a small cup of black coffee.

While waiting to be served she removed her gloves very leisurely and laid them beside her. Then she picked up a magazine and glanced through it, cutting the pages with a blunt edge of her knife. It was all very agreeable. The damask was even more spotless than it had seemed through the window, and the crystal more sparkling. There were quiet ladies and gentlemen, who did not notice her, lunching at the small tables like her own. A soft, pleasing strain of music could be heard, and a gentle breeze was blowing through the window. She tasted a bite, and she read a word or two, and she sipped the amber wine and wiggled her toes in the silk stockings. The price of it made no difference. She counted the money out to the waiter and left an extra coin on his tray, whereupon he bowed before her as before a princess of royal blood.

There was still money in her purse, and her next temptation presented itself in the shape of a matinee poster.

It was a little later when she entered the theatre, the play had begun and the house seemed to her to be packed. But there were vacant seats here and there, and into one of them she was ushered, between brilliantly dressed women who had gone there to kill time and eat candy and display their gaudy attire. There were many others who were there solely for the play and acting. It is safe to say there was no one present who bore quite the attitude which Mrs. Sommers did to her surroundings. She gathered in the whole—stage and players and people in one wide impression, and absorbed it and enjoyed it. She laughed at the comedy and wept—she and the gaudy woman next to her wept over the tragedy. And they talked a little together over it. And the gaudy woman wiped her eyes and sniffled on a tiny square of filmy, perfumed lace and passed little Mrs. Sommers her box of candy.

The play was over, the music ceased, the crowd filed out. It was like a dream ended. People scattered in all directions. Mrs. Sommers went to the corner and waited for the cable car.

A man with keen eyes, who sat opposite to her, seemed to like the study of her small, pale face. It puzzled him to decipher what he saw there. In truth, he saw nothing—unless he were wizard enough to detect a poignant wish, a powerful longing that the cable car would never stop anywhere, but go on and on with her forever.

A
Hunger Artist

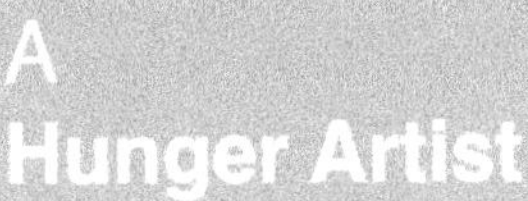

Franz Kafka

(Translation by Ian Johnston)

In the last decades interest in hunger artists has declined considerably. Whereas in earlier days there was good money to be earned putting on major productions of this sort under one's own management, nowadays that is totally impossible. Those were different times. Back then the hunger artist captured the attention of the entire city. From day to day while the fasting lasted, participation increased. Everyone wanted to see the hunger artist at least daily. During the final days there were people with subscription tickets who sat all day in front of the small barred cage. And there were even viewing hours at night, their impact heightened by torchlight. On fine days the cage was dragged out into the open air, and then the hunger artist was put on display particularly for the children. While for grown-ups the hunger artist was often merely a joke, something they participated in because it was fashionable, the children looked on amazed, their mouths open, holding each other's hands for safety, as he sat there on scattered straw—spurning a chair—in a black tights, looking pale, with his ribs sticking out prominently, sometimes nodding politely, answering questions with a forced smile, even sticking his arm out through the bars to let people feel how emaciated he was, but then completely sinking back into himself, so that he paid no attention to anything, not even to what was so important to him, the striking of the clock, which was the single furnishing in the cage, merely looking out in front of him with his eyes almost shut and now and then sipping from a tiny glass of water to moisten his lips.

Apart from the changing groups of spectators there were also constant observers chosen by the public—strangely enough they were usually butchers—who, always three at a time, were given the task of observing the hunger artist day and night, so that he didn't get something to eat in some secret manner. It was, however, merely a formality, introduced to reassure the masses, for those who understood knew well enough that during the period of fasting the hunger artist would never, under any circumstances, have eaten the slightest thing, not even if compelled by force. The honor of his art forbade it. Naturally, none of the watchers understood that. Sometimes there were nightly groups of watchers who carried out their vigil very laxly, deliberately sitting together in a distant corner and putting all their attention into playing cards there, clearly intending to allow the hunger artist a small refreshment, which, according to their way of thinking, he could get from some secret supplies. Nothing was more excruciating to the hunger artist than such watchers. They depressed him. They made his fasting terribly difficult.

   The Very Best Classic Short Stories

Sometimes he overcame his weakness and sang during
the time they were observing, for as long as he could
keep it up, to show people how unjust their suspicions
about him were. But that was little help. For then they
just wondered among themselves about his skill at being
able to eat even while singing. He much preferred the
observers who sat down right against the bars and,
not satisfied with the dim backlighting of the room,
illuminated him with electric flashlights. The glaring
light didn't bother him in the slightest. Generally he
couldn't sleep at all, and he could always doze under any
lighting and at any hour, even in an overcrowded, noisy
auditorium. With such observers, he was very happily
prepared to spend the entire night without sleeping. He
was very pleased to joke with them, to recount stories
from his nomadic life and then, in turn, to listen their
stories— doing everything just to keep them awake, so
that he could keep showing them once again that he
had nothing to eat in his cage and that he was fasting as
none of them could.

He was happiest, however, when morning came and
a lavish breakfast was brought for them at his own
expense, on which they hurled themselves with the ap-
petite of healthy men after a hard night's work without
sleep. True, there were still people who wanted to see
in this breakfast an unfair means of influencing the
observers, but that was going too far, and if they were

asked whether they wanted to undertake the observers' night shift for its own sake, without the breakfast, they excused themselves. But nonetheless they stood by their suspicions.

However, it was, in general, part of fasting that these doubts were inextricably associated with it. For, in fact, no one was in a position to spend time watching the hunger artist every day and night, so no one could know, on the basis of his own observation, whether this was a case of truly uninterrupted, flawless fasting. The hunger artist himself was the only one who could know that and, at the same time, the only spectator capable of being completely satisfied with his own fasting. But the reason he was never satisfied was something different. Perhaps it was not fasting at all which made him so very emaciated that many people, to their own regret, had to stay away from his performance, because they couldn't bear to look at him. For he was also so skeletal out of dissatisfaction with himself, because he alone knew something that even initiates didn't know—how easy it was to fast. It was the easiest thing in the world. About this he did not remain silent, but people did not believe him. At best they thought he was being modest. Most of them, however, believed he was a publicity seeker or a total swindler, for whom, at all events, fasting was easy, because he understood how to make it easy, and then had the nerve to half admit it. He had to accept

 The Very Best Classic Short Stories

all that. Over the years he had become accustomed to
it. But this dissatisfaction kept gnawing at his insides all
the time and never yet—and this one had to say to his
credit—had he left the cage of his own free will after
any period of fasting.

The impresario had set the maximum length of
time for the fast at forty days—he would never allow
the fasting go on beyond that point, not even in the
cosmopolitan cities. And, in fact, he had a good reason.
Experience had shown that for about forty days one
could increasingly whip up a city's interest by gradually
increasing advertising, but that then the people turned
away—one could demonstrate a significant decline in
popularity. In this respect, there were, of course, small
differences among different towns and among different
countries, but as a rule it was true that forty days was
the maximum length of time.

So then on the fortieth day the door of the cage—
which was covered with flowers— was opened, an
enthusiastic audience filled the amphitheatre, a military
band played, two doctors entered the cage, in order to
take the necessary measurements of the hunger artist,
the results were announced to the auditorium through a
megaphone, and finally two young ladies arrived, happy
about the fact that they were the ones who had just
been selected by lot, seeking to lead the hunger artist

down a couple of steps out of the cage, where on a small table a carefully chosen hospital meal was laid out. And at this moment the hunger artist always fought back. Of course, he still freely laid his bony arms in the helpful outstretched hands of the ladies bending over him, but he did not want to stand up. Why stop right now after forty days? He could have kept going for even longer, for an unlimited length of time. Why stop right now, when he was in his best form, indeed, not yet even in his best fasting form? Why did people want to rob him of the fame of fasting longer, not just so that he could become the greatest hunger artist of all time, which he probably was already, but also so that he could surpass himself in some unimaginable way, for he felt there were no limits to his capacity for fasting. Why did this crowd, which pretended to admire him so much, have so little patience with him? If he kept going and kept fasting longer, why would they not tolerate it? Then, too, he was tired and felt good sitting in the straw. Now he was supposed to stand up straight and tall and go to eat, something which, when he just imagined it, made him feel nauseous right away. With great difficulty he repressed mentioning this only out of consideration for the women. And he looked up into the eyes of these women, apparently so friendly but in reality so cruel, and shook his excessively heavy head on his feeble neck.

But then happened what always happened.

    The Very Best Classic Short Stories

The impresario came and in silence—the music made talking impossible—raised his arms over the hunger artist, as if inviting heaven to look upon its work here on the straw, this unfortunate martyr, something the hunger artist certainly was, only in a completely different sense, then grabbed the hunger artist around his thin waist, in the process wanting with his exaggerated caution to make people believe that here he had to deal with something fragile, and handed him over—not without secretly shaking him a little, so that the hunger artist's legs and upper body swung back and forth uncontrollably—to the women, who had in the meantime turned as pale as death. At this point, the hunger artist endured everything. His head lay on his chest—it was as if it had inexplicably rolled around and just stopped there— his body was arched back, his legs, in an impulse of self-preservation, pressed themselves together at the knees, but scraped the ground, as if they were not really on the floor but were looking for the real ground, and the entire weight of his body, admittedly very small, lay against one of the women, who appealed for help with flustered breath, for she had not imagined her post of honor would be like this, and then stretched her neck as far as possible, to keep her face from the least contact with the hunger artist, but then, when she couldn't manage this and her more fortunate companion didn't come to her assistance but trembled and remained content to hold in front of her the hunger artist's hand, that small bundle of knuckles, she broke into tears, to the delighted laughter of the auditorium, and had to be relieved by an attendant who had been standing ready for some time. Then came the meal. The impresario put a little food into mouth of the hunger artist, now half unconscious, as if fainting, and kept up a cheerful patter designed to divert attention away from the hunger artist's condition. Then a toast was proposed to the public, which was supposedly whispered to the impresario by the hunger artist, the orchestra confirmed everything with a great fanfare, people dispersed, and no one had the right to be dissatisfied with the event, no one except the hunger artist—he was always the only one.

He lived this way, taking small regular breaks, for many years, apparently in the spotlight, honored by the world, but for all that his mood was usually gloomy, and it kept growing gloomier all the time, because no one understood how to take him seriously. But how was he to find consolation? What was there left for him to wish for? And if a good-natured man who felt sorry for him ever wanted to explain to him that his sadness probably came from his fasting, then it could happen that the hunger artist responded with an outburst of rage and began to shake the bars like an animal, frightening everyone. But the impresario had a way of punishing moments like this, something he was happy

     The Very Best Classic Short Stories

to use. He would make an apology for the hunger artist to the assembled public, conceding that the irritability had been provoked only by his fasting, something quite intelligible to well-fed people and capable of excusing the behavior of the hunger artist without further explanation.

From there he would move on to speak about the equally hard to understand claim of the hunger artist that he could go on fasting for much longer than he was doing. He would praise the lofty striving, the good will, and the great self-denial no doubt contained in this claim, but then would try to contradict it simply by producing photographs, which were also on sale, for in the pictures one could see the hunger artist on the fortieth day of his fast, in bed, almost dead from exhaustion. Although the hunger artist was very familiar with this perversion of the truth, it always strained his nerves again and was too much for him. What was a result of the premature ending of the fast people were now proposing as its cause! It was impossible to fight against this lack of understanding, against this world of misunderstanding. In good faith he always listened eagerly to the impresario at the bars of his cage, but each time, once the photographs came out, he would let go of the bars and, with a sigh, sink back into the straw, and a reassured public could come up again and view him.

When those who had witnessed such scenes thought back on them a few years later, often they were unable to understand themselves. For in the meantime that change mentioned above had set it. It happened almost immediately. There may have been more profound reasons for it, but who bothered to discover what they were? At any rate, one day the pampered hunger artist saw himself abandoned by the crowd of pleasure seekers, who preferred to stream to other attractions. The impresario chased around half of Europe one more time with him, to see whether he could still re-discover the old interest here and there. It was all futile. It was as if a secret agreement against the fasting performances had developed everywhere. Naturally, it couldn't really have happened all at once, and people later remembered some things which in the days of intoxicating success they hadn't paid sufficient attention to, some inadequately suppressed indications, but now it was too late to do anything to counter them. Of course, it was certain that the popularity of fasting would return once more someday, but for those now alive that was no consolation. What was the hunger artist to do now? A man whom thousands of people had cheered on could not display himself in show booths at small fun fairs. The hunger artist was not only too old to take up a different profession, but was fanatically devoted to fasting more than anything else. So he said farewell to the impresario,

  The Very Best Classic Short Stories

an incomparable companion on his life's road, and let himself be hired by a large circus. In order to spare his own feelings, he didn't even look at the terms of his contract at all.

A large circus with its huge number of men, animals, and gimmicks, which are constantly being let go and replenished, can use anyone at any time, even a hunger artist, provided, of course, his demands are modest. Moreover, in this particular case it was not only the hunger artist himself wno was engaged, but also his old and famous name.

In fact, given the characteristic nature of his art, which was not diminished by his advancing age, one could never claim that a worn out artist, who no longer stood at the pinnacle of his ability, wanted to escape to a quiet position in the circus. On the contrary, the hunger artist declared that he could fast just as well as in earlier times—something that was entirely credible. Indeed, he even affirmed that if people would let him do what he wanted — and he was promised this without further ado—he would really now legitimately amaze the world for the first time, an assertion which, however, given the mood of the time, which the hunger artist in his enthusiasm easily overlooked, only brought smiles from the experts.

However, basically the hunger artist had not forgotten his sense of the way things really were, and he took it as self-evident that people would not set him and his cage up as the star attraction somewhere in the middle of the arena, but would move him outside in some other readily accessible spot near the animal stalls. Huge brightly painted signs surrounded the cage and announced what there was to look at there. During the intervals in the main performance, when the general public pushed out towards the menagerie in order to see the animals, they could hardly avoid moving past the hunger artist and stopping there a moment. They would perhaps have remained with him longer, if those pushing up behind them in the narrow passage way, who did not understand this pause on the way to the animal stalls they wanted to see, had not made a longer peaceful observation impossible. This was also the reason why the hunger artist began to tremble at these visiting hours, which he naturally used to long for as the main purpose of his life. In the early days he could hardly wait for the pauses in the performances. He had looked forward with delight to the crowd pouring around him, until he became convinced only too quickly—and even the most stubborn, almost deliberate self-deception could not hold out against the experience —that, judging by their intentions, most of these people were, again and again without exception, only visiting the menagerie.

   The Very Best Classic Short Stories

And this view from a distance still remained his most beautiful moment. For when they had come right up to him, he immediately got an earful from the shouting of the two steadily increasing groups, the ones who wanted to take their time looking at the hunger artist, not with any understanding but on a whim or from mere defiance—for him these ones were soon the more painful—and a second group of people whose only demand was to go straight to the animal stalls.

Once the large crowds had passed, the late comers would arrive, and although there was nothing preventing these people any more from sticking around for as long as they wanted, they rushed past with long strides, almost without a sideways glance, to get to the animals in time.

And it was an all-too-rare stroke of luck when the father of a family came by with his children, pointed his finger at the hunger artist, gave a detailed explanation about what was going on here, and talked of earlier years, when he had been present at similar but incomparably more magnificent performances, and then the children, because they had been inadequately prepared at school and in life, always stood around still uncomprehendingly. What was fasting to them? But nonetheless the brightness of the look in their searching eyes revealed something of new and more gracious times coming. Perhaps, the hunger artist said to himself sometimes, everything would be a little better if his location were not quite so near the animal stalls. That way it would be easy for people to make their choice, to say nothing of the fact that he was very upset and constantly depressed by the stink from the stalls, the animals' commotion at night, the pieces of raw meat dragged past him for the carnivorous beasts, and the roars at feeding time. But he did not dare to approach the administration about it. In any case, he had the animals to thank for the crowds of visitors among whom, here and there, there could be one destined for him. And who knew where they would hide him if he wished to remind them of his existence and, along with that, of the fact that, strictly speaking, he was only an obstacle on the way to the menagerie.

A small obstacle, at any rate, a constantly diminishing obstacle. People got used to the strange notion that in these times they would want to pay attention to a hunger artist, and with this habitual awareness the judgment on him was pronounced. He might fast as well as he could—and he did—but nothing could save him any more. People went straight past him. Try to explain the art of fasting to anyone! If someone doesn't feel it, then he cannot be made to understand it. The beautiful signs became dirty and illegible. People tore them down, and no one thought of replacing them.

    The Very Best Classic Short Stories

The small table with the number of days the fasting had lasted, which early on had been carefully renewed every day, remained unchanged for a long time, for after the first weeks the staff grew tired of even this small task. And so the hunger artist kept fasting on and on, as he once had dreamed about in earlier times, and he had no difficulty succeeding in achieving what he had predicted back then, but no one was counting the days—no one, not even the hunger artist himself, knew how great his achievement was by this point, and his heart grew heavy. And when once in a while a person strolling past stood there making fun of the old number and talking of a swindle, that was in a sense the stupidest lie which indifference and innate maliciousness could invent, for the hunger artist was not being deceptive—he was working honestly —but the world was cheating him of his reward.

Many days went by once more, and this, too, came to an end.

Finally the cage caught the attention of a supervisor, and he asked the attendant why they had left this perfectly useful cage standing here unused with rotting straw inside. Nobody knew, until one man, with the help of the table with the number on it, remembered the hunger artist. They pushed the straw around with a pole and found the hunger artist in there. "Are you still

fasting?" the supervisor asked. "When are you finally
going to stop?" "Forgive me everything," whispered the
hunger artist. Only the supervisor, who was pressing
his ear up against the cage, understood him. "Certainly," said the supervisor, tapping his forehead with his
finger in order to indicate to the spectators the state the
hunger artist was in, "we forgive you." "I always wanted
you to admire my fasting," said the hunger artist. "But
we do admire it," said the supervisor obligingly. "But
you shouldn't admire it," said the hunger artist. "Well
then, we don't admire it," said the supervisor, "but why
shouldn't we admire it?" "Because | had to fast. | can't
do anything else," said the hunger artist. "Just look at
you," said the supervisor, "why can't you do anything
else?" "Because," said the hunger artist, lifting his head
a little and, with his lips pursed as if for a kiss, speaking right into the supervisor's ear so that he wouldn't
miss anything, "because | couldn't find a food which |
enjoyed. If had found that, believe me, | would not have
made a spectacle of myself and would have eaten to my
heart's content, like you and everyone else." Those were
his last words, but in his failing eyes there was the firm,
if no longer proud, conviction that he was continuing
to fast.

"All right, tidy this up now," said the supervisor. And
they buried the hunger artist along with the straw. But
in his cage they put a young panther. Even for a person

with the dullest mind it was clearly refreshing to see this
wild animal throwing itself around in this cage, which
had been dreary for such a long time. It lacked nothing.
Without thinking about it for any length of time, the
guards brought the animal food. It enjoyed the taste
and never seemed to miss its freedom. This noble body,
equipped with everything necessary, almost to the point
of bursting, also appeared to carry freedom around with
it. That seem to be located somewhere or other in its
teeth, and its joy in living came with such strong passion
from its throat that it was not easy for spectators to
keep watching. But they controlled themselves, kept
pressing around the cage, and had no desire to move on.

THE
YELLOW PAINT

Robert Louis Stevenson

In a certain city there lived a physician who sold
yellow paint. This was of so singular a virtue that whoso
was bedaubed with it from head to heel was set free
from the dangers of life, and the bondage of sin, and
the fear of death for ever. So the physician said in his
prospectus; and so said all the citizens in the city; and
there was nothing more urgent in men's hearts than to
be properly painted themselves, and nothing they took
more delight in than to see others painted. There was
in the same city a young man of a very good family but
of a somewhat reckless life, who had reached the age of
manhood, and would have nothing to say to the paint:
"Tomorrow was soon enough," said he; and when the
morrow came he would still put it off. She might have
continued to do until his death; only, he had a friend
of about his own age and much of his own manners;
and this youth, taking a walk in the public street, with
not one fleck of paint upon his body, was suddenly run
down by a water–cart and cut off in the heyday of his
nakedness. This shook the other to the soul; so that I
never beheld a man more earnest to be painted; and on
the very same evening, in the presence of all his family,
to appropriate music, and himself weeping aloud, he
received three complete coats and a touch of varnish on
the top. The physician (who was himself affected even

to tears) protested he had never done a job so thorough.

Some two months afterwards, the young man was carried on a stretcher to the physician's house.

"What is the meaning of this?" he cried, as soon as the door was opened. "I was to be set free from all the dangers of life; and here have I been run down by that self–same water–cart, and my leg is broken."

"Dear me!" said the physician. "This is very sad. But I perceive I must explain to you the action of my paint. A broken bone is a mighty small affair at the worst of it; and it belongs to a class of accident to which my paint is quite inapplicable. Sin, my dear young friend, sin is the sole calamity that a wise man should apprehend; it is against sin that I have fitted you out; and when you come to be tempted, you will give me news of my paint."

"Oh!" said the young man, "I did not understand that, and it seems rather disappointing. But I have no doubt all is for the best; and in the meanwhile, I shall be obliged to you if you will set my leg."

"That is none of my business," said the physician; "but if your bearers will carry you round the corner to the surgeon's, I feel sure he will afford relief."

       The Very Best Classic Short Stories

Some three years later, the young man came running to the physician's house in a great perturbation. "What is the meaning of this?" he cried. "Here was I to be set free from the bondage of sin; and I have just committed forgery, arson and murder."

"Dear me," said the physician. "This is very serious. Off with your clothes at once." And as soon as the young man had stripped, he examined him from head to foot. "No," he cried with great relief, "there is not a flake broken. Cheer up, my young friend, your paint is as good as new."

"Good God!" cried the young man, "and what then can be the use of it?"

"Why," said the physician, "I perceive I must explain to you the nature of the action of my paint. It does not exactly prevent sin; it extenuates instead the painful consequences. It is not so much for this world, as for the next; it is not against life; in short, it is against death that I have fitted you out. And when you come to die, you will give me news of my paint."

"Oh!" cried the young man, "I had not understood that, and it seems a little disappointing. But there is no doubt all is for the best: and in the meanwhile, I shall be obliged if you will help me to undo the evil I have brought on innocent persons."

"That is none of my business," said the physician; "but if you will go round the corner to the police office, I feel sure it will afford you relief to give yourself up."

Six weeks later, the physician was called to the town gaol.

"What is the meaning of this?" cried the young man. "Here am I literally crusted with your paint; and I have broken my leg, and committed all the crimes in the calendar, and must be hanged tomorrow; and am in the meanwhile in a fear so extreme that I lack words to picture it."

"Dear me," said the physician. "This is really amazing. Well, well; perhaps, if you had not been painted, you would have been more frightened still."

THE
MODEL MILLIONAIRE

Oscar Wilde

Unless one is wealthy there is no use in being a charming fellow. Romance is the privilege of the rich, not the profession of the unemployed. The poor should be practical and prosaic. It is better to have a permanent income than to be fascinating. These are the great truths of modern life which Hughie Erskine never realised. Poor Hughie! Intellectually, we must admit, he was not of much importance. He never said a brilliant or even an ill-natured thing in his life. But then he was wonderfully good-looking, with his crisp brown hair, his clear-cut profile, and his grey eyes. He was as popular with men as he was with women and he had every accomplishment except that of making money. His father had bequeathed him his cavalry sword and a History of the Peninsular War in fifteen volumes. Hughie hung the first over his looking-glass, put the second on a shelf between Ruff's Guide and Bailey's Magazine, and lived on two hundred a year that an old aunt allowed him. He had tried everything. He had gone on the Stock Exchange for six months; but what was a butterfly to do among bulls and bears? He had been a tea-merchant for a little longer, but had soon tired of pekoe and souchong. Then he had tried selling dry sherry. That did not answer; the sherry was a little too dry. Ultimately he became nothing, a delightful, ineffectual young man with a perfect profile and no profession.

To make matters worse, he was in love. The girl he loved was Laura Merton, the daughter of a retired Colonel who had lost his temper and his digestion in India, and had never found either of them again. Laura adored him, and he was ready to kiss her shoe-strings. They were the handsomest couple in London, and had not a penny-piece between them. The Colonel was very fond of Hughie, but would not hear of any engagement.

'Come to me, my boy, when you have got ten thousand pounds of your own, and we will see about it,' he used to say; and Hughie looked very glum in those days, and had to go to Laura for consolation.

One morning, as he was on his way to Holland Park, where the Mertons lived, he dropped in to see a great friend of his, Alan Trevor. Trevor was a painter. Indeed, few people escape that nowadays. But he was also an artist, and artists are rather rare. Personally he was a strange rough fellow, with a freckled face and a red ragged beard. However, when he took up the brush he was a real master, and his pictures were eagerly sought after. He had been very much attracted by Hughie at first, it must be acknowledged, entirely on account of his personal charm. 'The only people a painter should know,' he used to say, 'are people who are bête and beautiful, people who are an artistic pleasure to look at and an intellectual repose to talk to. Men who are dandies and women who are darlings rule the world, at least they should do so.' However, after he got to know Hughie better, he liked him quite as much for his bright, buoyant spirits and his generous, reckless nature, and had given him the permanent entrée to his studio.

When Hughie came in he found Trevor putting the finishing touches to a wonderful life-size picture of a beggar-man. The beggar himself was standing on a raised platform in a corner of the studio. He was a wizened old man, with a face like wrinkled parchment, and a most piteous expression.

Over his shoulders was flung a coarse brown cloak, all tears and tatters; his thick boots were patched and cobbled, and with one hand he leant on a rough stick, while with the other he held out his battered hat for alms.

'What an amazing model!' whispered Hughie, as he shook hands with his friend.

'An amazing model?' shouted Trevor at the top of his voice; 'I should think so! Such beggars as he are not to be met with every day. A trouvaille, mon cher; a living Velasquez! My stars! what an etching Rembrandt would have made of him!'

'Poor old chap!' said Hughie, 'how miserable he looks! But I suppose, to you painters, his face is his fortune?'

'Certainly,' replied Trevor, 'you don't want a beggar to look happy, do you?'

'How much does a model get for sitting?' asked Hughie, as he found himself a comfortable seat on a divan.

'A shilling an hour.'

'And how much do you get for your picture, Alan?'

'Oh, for this I get two thousand!'

'Pounds?'

'Guineas. Painters, poets, and physicians always get guineas.'

'Well, I think the model should have a percentage,' cried Hughie, laughing; 'they work quite as hard as you do.'

'Nonsense, nonsense! Why, look at the trouble of laying on the paint alone, and standing all day long at one's easel! It's all very well, Hughie, for you to talk, but I assure you that there are moments when Art almost attains to the dignity of manual labour. But you mustn't chatter; I'm very busy. Smoke a cigarette, and keep quiet.'

After some time the servant came in, and told Trevor that the framemaker wanted to speak to him.

'Don't run away, Hughie,' he said, as he went out, 'I will be back in a moment.'

The old beggar-man took advantage of Trevor's absence to rest for a moment on a wooden bench that was behind him. He looked so forlorn and wretched that Hughie could not help pitying him, and felt in his pockets to see what money he had. All he could find was a sovereign and some coppers. 'Poor old fellow,' he thought to himself, 'he wants it more than I do, but it means no hansoms for a fortnight'; and he walked across the studio and slipped the sovereign into the beggar's hand.

The old man started, and a faint smile flitted across his withered lips. 'Thank you, sir,' he said, 'thank you.'

Then Trevor arrived, and Hughie took his leave, blushing a little at what he had done. He spent the day with Laura, got a charming scolding for his extravagance, and had to walk home.

That night he strolled into the Palette Club about eleven o'clock, and found Trevor sitting by himself in the smoking-room drinking hock and seltzer.

'Well, Alan, did you get the picture finished all right?' he said, as he lit his cigarette.

'Finished and framed, my boy!' answered Trevor; 'and, by the bye, you have made a conquest. That old model you saw is quite devoted to you. I had to tell him all about you - who you are, where you live, what your income is, what prospects you have - '

'My dear Alan,' cried Hughie, 'I shall probably find him waiting for me when I go home. But of course you are only joking. Poor old wretch! I wish I could do something for him. I think it is dreadful that any one should be so miserable. I have got heaps of old clothes at home - do you think he would care for any of them? Why, his rags were falling to bits.'

'But he looks splendid in them,' said Trevor. 'I wouldn't paint him in a frock coat for anything.

What you call rags I call romance. What seems poverty to you is picturesqueness to me. However, I'll tell him of your offer.'

'Alan,' said Hughie seriously, 'you painters are a heartless lot.'

'An artist's heart is his head,' replied Trevor; 'and

besides, our business is to realise the world as we see it, not to reform it as we know it. À chacun son métier. And now tell me how Laura is. The old model was quite interested in her.'

'You don't mean to say you talked to him about her?' said Hughie.

'Certainly I did. He knows all about the relentless colonel, the lovely Laura, and the £10,000.'

'You told that old beggar all my private affairs?' cried Hughie, looking very red and angry.

'My dear boy,' said Trevor, smiling, 'that old beggar, as you call him, is one of the richest men in Europe. He could buy all London to-morrow without overdrawing his account. He has a house in every capital, dines off gold plate, and can prevent Russia going to war when he chooses.'

'What on earth do you mean?' exclaimed Hughie.

'What I say,' said Trevor. 'The old man you saw to-day in the studio was Baron Hausberg. He is a great friend of mine, buys all my pictures and that sort of thing, and gave me a commission a month ago to paint him as a beggar. Que voulez-vous? La fantaisie d'un million-naire! And I must say he made a magnificent figure in his rags, or perhaps I should say in my rags; they are an old suit I got in Spain.'

'Baron Hausberg!' cried Hughie. 'Good heavens! I gave him a sovereign!' and he sank into an armchair the picture of dismay.

'Gave him a sovereign!' shouted Trevor, and he burst into a roar of laughter. 'My dear boy, you'll never see it again. Son affaire c'est l'argent des autres.'

'I think you might have told me, Alan,' said Hughie sulkily, 'and not have let me make such a fool of myself.'

'Well, to begin with, Hughie,' said Trevor, 'it never entered my mind that you went about distributing alms in that reckless way. I can understand your kissing a pretty model, but your giving a sovereign to an ugly one - by Jove, no! Besides, the fact is that I really was not at home to-day to any one; and when you came in I didn't know whether Hausberg would like his name mentioned. You know he wasn't in full dress.'

'What a duffer he must think me!' said Hughie.

'Not at all. He was in the highest spirits after you left; kept chuckling to himself and rubbing his old wrinkled hands together. I couldn't make out why he was so interested to know all about you; but I see it all now.

He'll invest your sovereign for you, Hughie, pay you the interest every six months, and have a capital story to tell after dinner.'

'I am an unlucky devil,' growled Hughie. 'The best thing I can do is to go to bed; and, my dear Alan, you mustn't tell any one. I shouldn't dare show my face in the Row.'

'Nonsense! It reflects the highest credit on your philanthropic spirit, Hughie. And don't run away. Have another cigarette, and you can talk about Laura as much as you like.'

However, Hughie wouldn't stop, but walked home, feeling very unhappy, and leaving Alan Trevor in fits of laughter.

The next morning, as he was at breakfast, the servant brought him up a card on which was written, 'Monsieur Gustave Naudin, de la part de M. le Baron Hausberg.'

'I suppose he has come for an apology,' said Hughie to himself; and he told the servant to show the visitor up.

An old gentleman with gold spectacles and grey hair came into the room, and said, in a slight French accent, 'Have I the honour of addressing Monsieur Erskine?'

Hughie bowed.

'I have come from Baron Hausberg,' he continued. 'The Baron - '

'I beg, sir, that you will offer him my sincerest apologies,' stammered Hughie.

'The Baron,' said the old gentleman with a smile, 'has commissioned me to bring you this letter'; and he extended a sealed envelope.

On the outside was written, 'A wedding present to Hugh Erskine and Laura Merton, from an old beggar,' and inside was a cheque for £10,000.

When they were married Alan Trevor was the best man, and the Baron made a speech at the wedding breakfast.

'Millionaire models,' remarked Alan, 'are rare enough; but, by Jove, model millionaires are rarer still!'

The End.

THE
SINGING LESSON

Katherine Mansfield

With despair—cold, sharp despair—buried deep in her heart like a wicked knife, Miss Meadows, in cap and gown and carrying a little baton, trod the cold corridors that led to the music hall. Girls of all ages, rosy from the air, and bubbling over with that gleeful excitement that comes from running to school on a fine autumn morning, hurried, skipped, fluttered by; from the hollow class-rooms came a quick drumming of voices; a bell rang; a voice like a bird cried, "Muriel." And then there came from the staircase a tremendous knock-knock-knocking. Some one had dropped her dumbbells.

The Science Mistress stopped Miss Meadows.

"Good mor-ning," she cried, in her sweet, affected drawl. "Isn't it cold? It might be win-ter."

Miss Meadows, hugging the knife, stared in hatred at the Science Mistress. Everything about her was sweet, pale, like honey. You would not have been surprised to see a bee caught in the tangles of that yellow hair.

"It is rather sharp," said Miss Meadows, grimly.

The other smiled her sugary smile.

"You look fro-zen," said she. Her blue eyes opened

wide; there came a mocking light in them. (Had she noticed anything?)

"Oh, not quite as bad as that," said Miss Meadows, and she gave the Science Mistress, in exchange for her smile, a quick grimace and passed on....

Forms Four, Five, and Six were assembled in the music hall. The noise was deafening. On the platform, by the piano, stood Mary Beazley, Miss Meadows' favourite, who played accompaniments. She was turning the music stool. When she saw Miss Meadows she gave a loud, warning "Sh-sh! girls!" and Miss Meadows, her hands thrust in her sleeves, the baton under her arm, strode down the centre aisle, mounted the steps, turned sharply, seized the brass music stand, planted it in front of her, and gave two sharp taps with her baton for silence.

"Silence, please! Immediately!" and, looking at nobody, her glance swept over that sea of coloured flannel blouses, with bobbing pink faces and hands, quivering butterfly hair-bows, and music-books outspread. She knew perfectly well what they were thinking. "Meady is in a wax." Well, let them think it! Her eyelids quivered; she tossed her head, defying them. What could the thoughts of those creatures matter to some one who stood there bleeding to death, pierced to the heart, to the heart, by such a letter—

    The Very Best Classic Short Stories

... "I feel more and more strongly that our marriage would be a mistake. Not that I do not love you. I love you as much as it is possible for me to love any woman, but, truth to tell, I have come to the conclusion that I am not a marrying man, and the idea of settling down fills me with nothing but—" and the word "disgust" was scratched out lightly and "regret" written over the top.

Basil! Miss Meadows stalked over to the piano. And Mary Beazley, who was waiting for this moment, bent forward; her curls fell over her cheeks while she breathed, "Good morning, Miss Meadows," and she motioned towards rather than handed to her mistress a beautiful yellow chrysanthemum. This little ritual of the flower had been gone through for ages and ages, quite a term and a half. It was as much part of the lesson as opening the piano. But this morning, instead of taking it up, instead of tucking it into her belt while she leant over Mary and said, "Thank you, Mary. How very nice! Turn to page thirty-two," what was Mary's horror when Miss Meadows totally ignored the chrysanthemum, made no reply to her greeting, but said in a voice of ice, "Page fourteen, please, and mark the accents well."

Staggering moment! Mary blushed until the tears stood in her eyes, but Miss Meadows was gone back to the music stand; her voice rang through the music hall.

"Page fourteen. We will begin with page fourteen. 'A Lament.' Now, girls, you ought to know it by this time. We shall take it all together; not in parts, all together. And without expression. Sing it, though, quite simply, beating time with the left hand."

She raised the baton; she tapped the music stand twice. Down came Mary on the opening chord; down came all those left hands, beating the air, and in chimed those young, mournful voices:—

> Fast! Ah, too Fast Fade the Ro-o-ses of Pleasure;
> Soon Autumn yields unto Wi-i-nter Drear.
> Fleetly! Ah, Fleetly Mu-u-sic's Gay Measure
> Passes away from the Listening Ear.

Good Heavens, what could be more tragic than that lament! Every note was a sigh, a sob, a groan of awful mournfulness. Miss Meadows lifted her arms in the wide gown and began conducting with both hands. "... I feel more and more strongly that our marriage would be a mistake...." she beat. And the voices cried: *Fleetly! Ah, Fleetly*. What could have possessed him to write such a letter! What could have led up to it! It came out of nothing. His last letter had been all about a fumed-oak bookcase he had bought for "our" books, and a "natty little hall-stand" he had seen, "a very neat affair with a carved owl on a bracket, holding three hat-brushes in its claws." How she had smiled at that! So like a man to think one needed three hat-brushes! *From the Listening Ear*, sang the voices.

"Once again," said Miss Meadows. "But this time in parts. Still without expression." *Fast! Ah, too Fast.* With the gloom of the contraltos added, one could scarcely help shuddering. *Fade the Roses of Pleasure.* Last time he had come to see her, Basil had worn a rose in his button-hole. How handsome he had looked in that bright blue suit, with that dark red rose! And he knew it, too. He couldn't help knowing it. First he stroked his hair, then his moustache; his teeth gleamed when he smiled.

"The headmaster's wife keeps on asking me to dinner. It's a perfect nuisance. I never get an evening to myself in that place."

"But can't you refuse?"

"Oh, well, it doesn't do for a man in my position to be unpopular."

Music's Gay Measure, wailed the voices. The willow trees, outside the high, narrow windows, waved in the wind. They had lost half their leaves. The tiny ones that clung wriggled like fishes caught on a line. "... I am not a marrying man...." The voices were silent; the piano waited.

"Quite good," said Miss Meadows, but still in such a strange, stony tone that the younger girls began to feel positively frightened. "But now that we know it, we shall take it with expression. As much expression as you can put into it. Think of the words, girls. Use your imaginations. *Fast! Ah, too Fast*," cried Miss Meadows. "That ought to break out—a loud, strong *forte*—a lament. And then in the second line, *Winter Drear*, make that *Drear* sound as if a cold wind were blowing through it. *Dre-ear!*" said she so awfully that Mary Beazley, on the music stool, wriggled her spine. "The third line should be one crescendo. *Fleetly! Ah, Fleetly Music's Gay Measure*. Breaking on the first word of the last line, *Passes*. And then on the word, *Away*, you must begin to die... to fade... until *The Listening Ear* is nothing more than a faint whisper.... You can slow down as much as you like almost on the last line. Now, please."

Again the two light taps; she lifted her arms again. *Fast! Ah, too Fast*. "... and the idea of settling down fills me with nothing but disgust—" Disgust was what he had written. That was as good as to say their engagement was definitely broken off. Broken off! Their engagement! People had been surprised enough that she had got engaged. The Science Mistress would not believe it at first. But nobody had been as surprised as she. She was thirty. Basil was twenty-five. It had been a miracle, simply a miracle, to hear him say, as they walked home from church that very dark night, "You know, somehow or other, I've got fond of you." And he had taken hold of the end of her ostrich feather boa. *Passes away from the Listening Ear.*

"Repeat! Repeat!" said Miss Meadows. "More expression, girls! Once more!"

Fast! Ah, too Fast. The older girls were crimson; some of the younger ones began to cry. Big spots of rain blew against the windows, and one could hear the willows whispering, "... not that I do not love you...."

"But, my darling, if you love me," thought Miss Meadows, "I don't mind how much it is. Love me as little as you like." But she knew he didn't love her. Not to have cared enough to scratch out that word "disgust," so that she couldn't read it! *Soon Autumn yields unto Winter Drear.* She would have to leave the school, too. She could never face the Science Mistress or the girls after it got known. She would have to disappear somewhere. *Passes away.* The voices began to die, to fade, to whisper... to vanish....

Suddenly the door opened. A little girl in blue walked fussily up the aisle, hanging her head, biting her lips, and twisting the silver bangle on her red little wrist. She came up the steps and stood before Miss Meadows.

"Well, Monica, what is it?"

"Oh, if you please, Miss Meadows," said the little girl, gasping, "Miss Wyatt wants to see you in the mistress's room."

"Very well," said Miss Meadows. And she called to the girls, "I shall put you on your honour to talk quietly while I am away." But they were too subdued to do anything else. Most of them were blowing their noses.

The corridors were silent and cold; they echoed to Miss Meadows' steps. The head mistress sat at her desk. For a moment she did not look up. She was as usual disentangling her eyeglasses, which had got caught in her lace tie. "Sit down, Miss Meadows," she said very kindly. And then she picked up a pink envelope from the blotting-pad. "I sent for you just now because this telegram has come for you."

"A telegram for me, Miss Wyatt?"

Basil! He had committed suicide, decided Miss Meadows. Her hand flew out, but Miss Wyatt held the telegram back a moment. "I hope it's not bad news," she said, so more than kindly. And Miss Meadows tore it open.

"Pay no attention to letter, must have been mad,

bought hat-stand to-day—Basil," she read. She couldn't take her eyes off the telegram.

"I do hope it's nothing very serious," said Miss Wyatt, leaning forward.

"Oh, no, thank you, Miss Wyatt," blushed Miss Meadows. "It's nothing bad at all. It's"—and she gave an apologetic little laugh—"it's from my *fiancé* saying that... saying that—" There was a pause. "I *see*," said Miss Wyatt. And another pause. Then—"You've fifteen minutes more of your class, Miss Meadows, haven't you?"

"Yes, Miss Wyatt." She got up. She half ran towards the door.

"Oh, just one minute, Miss Meadows," said Miss Wyatt. "I must say I don't approve of my teachers having telegrams sent to them in school hours, unless in case of very bad news, such as death," explained Miss Wyatt, "or a very serious accident, or something to that effect. Good news, Miss Meadows, will always keep, you know."

On the wings of hope, of love, of joy, Miss Meadows sped back to the music hall, up the aisle, up the steps, over to the piano.

"Page thirty-two, Mary," she said, "page thirty-two,"

and, picking up the yellow chrysanthemum, she held
it to her lips to hide her smile. Then she turned to the
girls, rapped with her baton: "Page thirty-two, girls.
Page thirty-two."

> We come here To-day with Flowers o'erladen,
> With Baskets of Fruit and Ribbons to boot,
> To-oo Congratulate ...

"Stop! Stop!" cried Miss Meadows. "This is awful.
This is dreadful." And she beamed at her girls. "What's
the matter with you all? Think, girls, think of what
you're singing. Use your imaginations. *With Flowers
o'erladen. Baskets of Fruit and Ribbons to boot. And
Congratulate.*" Miss Meadows broke off. "Don't look
so doleful, girls. It ought to sound warm, joyful, eager.
Congratulate. Once more. Quickly. All together. Now
then!"

And this time Miss Meadows' voice sounded over all
the other voices—full, deep, glowing with expression.

THE
AMBITIOUS GUEST

Nathaniel Hawthorne

One September night a family had gathered round their hearth, and piled it high with the driftwood of mountain streams, the dry cones of the pine, and the splintered ruins of great trees that had come crashing down the precipice. Up the chimney roared the fire, and brightened the room with its broad blaze. The faces of the father and mother had a sober gladness; the children laughed; the eldest daughter was the image of Happiness at seventeen; and the aged grandmother, who sat knitting in the warmest place, was the image of Happiness grown old. They had found the "herb, heart's-ease," in the bleakest spot of all New England. This family were situated in the Notch of the White Hills, where the wind was sharp throughout the year, and pitilessly cold in the winter,--giving their cottage all its fresh inclemency before it descended on the valley of the Saco. They dwelt in a cold spot and a dangerous one; for a mountain towered above their heads, so steep, that the stones would often rumble down its sides and startle them at midnight.

The daughter had just uttered some simple jest that filled them all with mirth, when the wind came through the Notch and seemed to pause before their cot-tage--rattling the door, with a sound of wailing and lamentation, before it passed into the valley. For a moment it saddened them, though there was nothing unusual in the tones. But the family were glad again when they perceived that the latch was lifted by some traveller, whose footsteps had been unheard amid the dreary blast which heralded his approach, and wailed as he was entering, and went moaning away from the door.

Though they dwelt in such a solitude, these people held daily converse with the world. The romantic pass of the Notch is a great artery, through which the life-blood of internal commerce is continually throbbing between Maine, on one side, and the Green Mountains and the shores of the St. Lawrence, on the other. The stage-coach always drew up before the door of the cottage. The wayfarer, with no companion but his staff, paused here to exchange a word, that the sense of loneliness might not utterly overcome him ere he could pass through the cleft of the mountain, or reach the first house in the valley. And here the teamster, on his way to Portland market, would put up for the night; and, if a bachelor, might sit an hour beyond the usual bedtime, and steal a kiss from the mountain maid at parting. It was one of those primitive taverns where the traveller pays only for food and lodging, but meets with a homely kindness beyond all price. When the footsteps were heard, therefore, between the outer door and the inner one, the whole family rose up, grandmother, children

 The Very Best Classic Short Stories

and all, as if about to welcome some one who belonged to them, and whose fate was linked with theirs.

The door was opened by a young man. His face at first wore the melancholy expression, almost despondency, of one who travels a wild and bleak road, at nightfall and alone, but soon brightened up when he saw the kindly warmth of his reception. He felt his heart spring forward to meet them all, from the old woman, who wiped a chair with her apron, to the little child that held out its arms to him. One glance and smile placed the stranger on a footing of innocent familiarity with the eldest daughter.

"Ah, this fire is the right thing!" cried he; "especially when there is such a pleasant circle round it. I am quite benumbed; for the Notch is just like the pipe of a great pair of bellows; it has blown a terrible blast in my face all the way from Bartlett."

"Then you are going towards Vermont?" said the master of the house, as he helped to take a light knapsack off the young man's shoulders.

"Yes; to Burlington, and far enough beyond," replied he. "I meant to have been at Ethan Crawford's to-night; but a pedestrian lingers along such a road as this. It is no matter; for, when I saw this good fire, and all your cheerful faces, I felt as if you had kindled it on purpose for me, and were waiting my arrival. So I shall sit down among you, and make myself at home."

The frank-hearted stranger had just drawn his chair to the fire when something like a heavy footstep was heard without, rushing down the steep side of the mountain, as with long and rapid strides, and taking such a leap in passing the cottage as to strike the opposite precipice. The family held their breath, because they knew the sound, and their guest held his by instinct.

"The old mountain has thrown a stone at us, for fear we should forget him," said the landlord, recovering himself. "He sometimes nods his head and threatens to come down; but we are old neighbors, and agree together pretty well upon the whole. Besides we have a sure place of refuge hard by if he should be coming in good earnest."

Let us now suppose the stranger to have finished his supper of bear's meat; and, by his natural felicity of manner, to have placed himself on a footing of kindness with the whole family, so that they talked as freely together as if he belonged to their mountain brood. He was of a proud, yet gentle spirit--haughty and reserved among the rich and great; but ever ready to stoop his head to the lowly cottage door, and be like a brother or a son at the poor man's fireside. In the household of the

 The Very Best Classic Short Stories

Notch he found warmth and simplicity of feeling, the pervading intelligence of New England, and a poetry of native growth, which they had gathered when they little thought of it from the mountain peaks and chasms, and at the very threshold of their romantic and dangerous abode. He had travelled far and alone; his whole life, indeed, had been a solitary path; for, with the lofty caution of his nature, he had kept himself apart from those who might otherwise have been his companions. The family, too, though so kind and hospitable, had that consciousness of unity among themselves, and separation from the world at large, which, in every domestic circle, should still keep a holy place where no stranger may intrude. But this evening a prophetic sympathy impelled the refined and educated youth to pour out his heart before the simple mountaineers, and constrained them to answer him with the same free confidence. And thus it should have been. Is not the kindred of a common fate a closer tie than that of birth?

The secret of the young man's character was a high and abstracted ambition. He could have borne to live an undistinguished life, but not to be forgotten in the grave. Yearning desire had been transformed to hope; and hope, long cherished, had become like certainty, that, obscurely as he journeyed now, a glory was to beam on all his pathway,--though not, perhaps, while he was treading it. But when posterity should gaze back into the gloom of what was now the present, they would trace the brightness of his footsteps, brightening as meaner glories faded, and confess that a gifted one had passed from his cradle to his tomb with none to recognize him.

"As yet," cried the stranger--his cheek glowing and his eye flashing with enthusiasm--"as yet, I have done nothing. Were I to vanish from the earth to-morrow, none would know so much of me as you: that a nameless youth came up at nightfall from the valley of the Saco, and opened his heart to you in the evening, and passed through the Notch by sunrise, and was seen no more. Not a soul would ask, 'Who was he? Whither did the wanderer go?' But I cannot die till I have achieved my destiny. Then, let Death come! I shall have built my monument!"

There was a continual flow of natural emotion, gushing forth amid abstracted reverie, which enabled the family to understand this young man's sentiments, though so foreign from their own. With quick sensibility of the ludicrous, he blushed at the ardor into which he had been betrayed.

"You laugh at me," said he, taking the eldest daughter's hand, and laughing himself. "You think my ambition as nonsensical as if I were to freeze myself to death on the

 The Very Best Classic Short Stories

top of Mount Washington, only that people might spy
at me from the country round about. And, truly, that
would be a noble pedestal for a man's statue!"

"It is better to sit here by this fire," answered the girl,
blushing, "and be comfortable and contented, though
nobody thinks about us."

"I suppose," said her father, after a fit of musing, "there
is something natural in what the young man says; and
if my mind had been turned that way, I might have felt
just the same. It is strange, wife, how his talk has set my
head running on things that are pretty certain never to
come to pass."

"Perhaps they may," observed the wife. "Is the man
thinking what he will do when he is a widower?"

"No, no!" cried he, repelling the idea with reproachful
kindness. "When I think of your death, Esther, I think
of mine, too. But I was wishing we had a good farm
in Bartlett, or Bethlehem, or Littleton, or some other
township round the White Mountains; but not where
they could tumble on our heads. I should want to stand
well with my neighbors and be called Squire, and sent
to General Court for a term or two; for a plain, honest
man may do as much good there as a lawyer. And when
I should be grown quite an old man, and you an old
woman, so as not to be long apart, I might die happy

enough in my bed, and leave you all crying around me. A slate gravestone would suit me as well as a marble one--with just my name and age, and a verse of a hymn, and something to let people know that I lived an honest man and died a Christian."

"There now!" exclaimed the stranger; "it is our nature to desire a monument, be it slate or marble, or a pillar of granite, or a glorious memory in the universal heart of man."

"We're in a strange way, to-night," said the wife, with tears in her eyes. "They say it's a sign of something, when folks' minds go a wandering so. Hark to the children!"

They listened accordingly. The younger children had been put to bed in another room, but with an open door between, so that they could be heard talking busily among themselves. One and all seemed to have caught the infection from the fireside circle, and were outvying each other in wild wishes, and childish projects of what they would do when they came to be men and women. At length a little boy, instead of addressing his brothers and sisters, called out to his mother.

"I'll tell you what I wish, mother," cried he. "I want you and father and grandma'm, and all of us, and the stranger too, to start right away, and go and take a drink out of the basin of the Flume!"

Nobody could help laughing at the child's notion of leaving a warm bed, and dragging them from a cheerful fire, to visit the basin of the Flume,--a brook, which tumbles over the precipice, deep within the Notch. The boy had hardly spoken when a wagon rattled along the road, and stopped a moment before the door. It appeared to contain two or three men, who were cheering their hearts with the rough chorus of a song, which resounded, in broken notes, between the cliffs, while the singers hesitated whether to continue their journey or put up here for the night.

"Father," said the girl, "they are calling you by name."

But the good man doubted whether they had really called him, and was unwilling to show himself too solicitous of gain by inviting people to patronize his house. He therefore did not hurry to the door; and the lash being soon applied, the travellers plunged into the Notch, still singing and laughing, though their music and mirth came back drearily from the heart of the mountain.

"There, mother!" cried the boy, again. "They'd have given us a ride to the Flume."

Again they laughed at the child's pertinacious fancy for a night ramble. But it happened that a light cloud passed over the daughter's spirit; she looked gravely into the fire, and drew a breath that was almost a sigh. It forced its way, in spite of a little struggle to repress it. Then starting and blushing, she looked quickly round the circle, as if they had caught a glimpse into her bosom. The stranger asked what she had been thinking of.

"Nothing," answered she, with a downcast smile. "Only I felt lonesome just then."

"Oh, I have always had a gift of feeling what is in other people's hearts," said he, half seriously. "Shall I tell the secrets of yours? For I know what to think when a young girl shivers by a warm hearth, and complains of lonesomeness at her mother's side. Shall I put these feelings into words?"

"They would not be a girl's feelings any longer if they could be put into words," replied the mountain nymph, laughing, but avoiding his eye.

All this was said apart. Perhaps a germ of love was springing in their hearts, so pure that it might blossom in Paradise, since it could not be matured on earth; for women worship such gentle dignity as his; and the proud, contemplative, yet kindly soul is oftenest captivated by simplicity like hers. But while they spoke softly, and he was watching the happy sadness, the lightsome shadows, the shy yearnings of a maiden's nature, the wind through the Notch took a deeper and drearier sound. It seemed, as the fanciful stranger said, like the choral strain of the spirits of the blast, who in old Indian times had their dwelling among these mountains, and made their heights and recesses a sacred region. There was a wail along the road, as if a funeral were passing. To chase away the gloom, the family threw pine branches on their fire, till the dry leaves crackled and the flame arose, discovering once again a scene of peace and humble happiness. The light hovered about them fondly, and caressed them all. There were the little faces of the children, peeping from their bed apart and here the father's frame of strength, the mother's subdued and careful mien, the high-browed youth, the budding girl, and the good old grandam, still knitting in the warmest place. The aged woman looked up from her task, and, with fingers ever busy, was the next to speak.

"Old folks have their notions," said she, "as well as young ones. You've been wishing and planning; and letting your heads run on one thing and another, till you've set my mind a wandering too. Now what should an old woman wish for, when she can go but a step or two before she comes to her grave? Children, it will haunt me night and day till I tell you."

"What is it, mother?" cried the husband and wife at once.

Then the old woman, with an air of mystery which drew the circle closer round the fire, informed them that she had provided her graveclothes some years before,--a nice linen shroud, a cap with a muslin ruff, and everything of a finer sort than she had worn since her wedding day. But this evening an old superstition had strangely recurred to her. It used to be said, in her younger days, that if anything were amiss with a corpse, if only the ruff were not smooth, or the cap did not set right, the corpse in the coffin and beneath the clods would strive to put up its cold hands and arrange it. The bare thought made her nervous.

"Don't talk so, grandmother!" said the girl, shuddering.

"Now,"--continued the old woman, with singular earnestness, yet smiling strangely at her own folly,--"I want one of you, my children--when your mother is dressed and in the coffin--I want one of you to hold a looking-glass over my face. Who knows but I may take a glimpse at myself, and see whether all's right?"

"Old and young, we dream of graves and monuments," murmured the stranger youth. "I wonder how mariners feel when the ship is sinking, and they, unknown and undistinguished, are to be buried together in the ocean--that wide and nameless sepulchre?"

     The Very Best Classic Short Stories

For a moment, the old woman's ghastly conception so engrossed the minds of her hearers that a sound abroad in the night, rising like the roar of a blast, had grown broad, deep, and terrible, before the fated group were conscious of it. The house and all within it trembled; the foundations of the earth seemed to be shaken, as if this awful sound were the peal of the last trump. Young and old exchanged one wild glance, and remained an instant, pale, affrighted, without utterance, or power to move. Then the same shriek burst simultaneously from all their lips.

"The Slide! The Slide!"

The simplest words must intimate, but not portray, the unutterable horror of the catastrophe. The victims rushed from their cottage, and sought refuge in what they deemed a safer spot--where, in contemplation of such an emergency, a sort of barrier had been reared. Alas! they had quitted their security, and fled right into the pathway of destruction. Down came the whole side of the mountain, in a cataract of ruin. Just before it reached the house, the stream broke into two branches--shivered not a window there, but overwhelmed the whole vicinity, blocked up the road, and annihilated everything in its dreadful course. Long ere the thunder of the great Slide had ceased to roar among the mountains, the mortal agony had been endured, and the victims were at peace. Their bodies were never found.

The next morning, the light smoke was seen steal-
ing from the cottage chimney up the mountain side.
Within, the fire was yet smouldering on the hearth, and
the chairs in a circle round it, as if the inhabitants had
but gone forth to view the devastation of the Slide, and
would shortly return, to thank Heaven for their miracu-
lous escape. All had left separate tokens, by which those
who had known the family were made to shed a tear
for each. Who has not heard their name? The story has
been told far and wide, and will forever be a legend of
these mountains. Poets have sung their fate.

There were circumstances which led some to suppose
that a stranger had been received into the cottage on
this awful night, and had shared the catastrophe of all
its inmates. Others denied that there were sufficient
grounds for such a conjecture. Woe for the high-souled
youth, with his dream of Earthly Immortality! His
name and person utterly unknown; his history, his way
of life, his plans, a mystery never to be solved, his death
and his existence equally a doubt! Whose was the agony
of that death moment?

   The Very Best Classic Short Stories

TOBERMORY

Saki

It was a chill, rain-washed afternoon of a late August day, that indefinite season when partridges are still in security or cold storage, and there is nothing to hunt—unless one is bounded on the north by the Bristol Channel, in which case one may lawfully gallop after fat red stags. Lady Blemley's house-party was not bounded on the north by the Bristol Channel, hence there was a full gathering of her guests round the tea-table on this particular afternoon. And, in spite of the blankness of the season and the triteness of the occasion, there was no trace in the company of that fatigued restlessness which means a dread of the pianola and a subdued hankering for auction bridge. The undisguised open-mouthed attention of the entire party was fixed on the homely negative personality of Mr. Cornelius Appin. Of all her guests, he was the one who had come to Lady Blemley with the vaguest reputation. Some one had said he was "clever," and he had got his invitation in the moderate expectation, on the part of his hostess, that some portion at least of his cleverness would be contributed to the general entertainment. Until tea-time that day she had been unable to discover in what direction, if any, his cleverness lay. He was neither a wit nor a croquet champion, a hypnotic force nor a begetter of amateur theatricals. Neither did his exterior suggest the sort of man in whom women are willing to pardon a generous measure of mental deficiency. He had subsided into mere Mr. Appin, and the Cornelius seemed a piece of transparent baptismal bluff. And now he was claiming to have launched on the world a discovery beside which the invention of gunpowder, of the printing-press, and of steam locomotion were inconsiderable trifles. Science had made bewildering strides in many directions during recent decades, but this thing seemed to belong to the domain of miracle rather than to scientific achievement.

"And do you really ask us to believe," Sir Wilfrid was saying, "that you have discovered a means for instructing animals in the art of human speech, and that dear old Tobermory has proved your first successful pupil?"

"It is a problem at which I have worked for the last seventeen years," said Mr. Appin, "but only during the last eight or nine months have I been rewarded with glimmerings of success. Of course I have experimented with thousands of animals, but latterly only with cats, those wonderful creatures which have assimilated themselves so marvelously with our civilization while retaining all their highly developed feral instincts. Here and there among cats one comes across an outstanding superior intellect, just as one does among the ruck of human beings, and when I made the acquaintance of Tobermory a week ago I saw at once that I was in contact with a "Beyond-cat" of extraordinary intelligence. I had gone far along the road to success in recent experiments; with Tobermory, as you call him, I have reached the goal."

Mr. Appin concluded his remarkable statement in a voice which he strove to divest of a triumphant inflection. No one said "Rats," though Clovis's lips moved in a monosyllabic contortion, which probably invoked those rodents of disbelief.

"And do you mean to say," asked Miss Resker, after a slight pause, "that you have taught Tobermory to say and understand easy sentences of one syllable?"

"My dear Miss Resker," said the wonder-worker patiently, "one teaches little children and savages and backward adults in that piecemeal fashion; when one has once solved the problem of making a beginning with an animal of highly developed intelligence one has no need for those halting methods. Tobermory can speak our language with perfect correctness."

This time Clovis very distinctly said, "Beyond-rats!" Sir Wilfred was more polite but equally sceptical.

"Hadn't we better have the cat in and judge for ourselves?" suggested Lady Blemley.

Sir Wilfred went in search of the animal, and the company settled themselves down to the languid expectation of witnessing some more or less adroit drawing-room ventriloquism.

In a minute Sir Wilfred was back in the room, his face white beneath its tan and his eyes dilated with excitement.

"By Gad, it's true!"

His agitation was unmistakably genuine, and his hearers started forward in a thrill of wakened interest.

Collapsing into an armchair he continued breathlessly:

"I found him dozing in the smoking-room, and called out to him to come for his tea. He blinked at me in his usual way, and I said, 'Come on, Toby; don't keep us waiting' and, by Gad! he drawled out in a most horribly natural voice that he'd come when he dashed well pleased! I nearly jumped out of my skin!"

Appin had preached to absolutely incredulous hearers; Sir Wilfred's statement carried instant conviction. A Babel-like chorus of startled exclamation arose, amid which the scientist sat mutely enjoying the first fruit of his stupendous discovery.

In the midst of the clamour Tobermory entered the room and made his way with velvet tread and studied unconcern across the group seated round the tea-table.

A sudden hush of awkwardness and constraint fell on the company. Somehow there seemed an element of embarrassment in addressing on equal terms a domestic cat of acknowledged dental ability.

"Will you have some milk, Tobermory?" asked Lady Blemley in a rather strained voice.

"I don't mind if I do," was the response, couched in a tone of even indifference. A shiver of suppressed excitement went through the listeners, and Lady Blemley might be excused for pouring out the saucerful of milk rather unsteadily.

"I'm afraid I've spilt a good deal of it," she said apologetically.

"After all, it's not my Axminster," was Tobermory's rejoinder.

Another silence fell on the group, and then Miss Resker, in her best district-visitor manner, asked if the human language had been difficult to learn. Tobermory looked squarely at her for a moment and then fixed his gaze serenely on the middle distance. It was obvious that boring questions lay outside his scheme of life.

"What do you think of human intelligence?" asked Mavis Pellington lamely.

"Of whose intelligence in particular?" asked Tobermory coldly.

"Oh, well, mine for instance," said Mavis with a feeble laugh.

"You put me in an embarrassing position," said Tobermory, whose tone and attitude certainly did not suggest a shred of embarrassment. "When your inclusion in this house-party was suggested Sir Wilfrid protested that you were the most brainless woman of his acquaintance, and that there was a wide distinction between hospitality and the care of the feeble-minded. Lady Blemley replied that your lack of brain-power was the precise quality which had earned you your invitation, as you were the only person she could think of who might be idiotic enough to buy their old car. You know, the one they call 'The Envy of Sisyphus,' because it goes quite nicely up-hill if you push it."

Lady Blemley's protestations would have had greater effect if she had not casually suggested to Mavis only that morning that the car in question would be just the thing for her down at her Devonshire home.

Major Barfield plunged in heavily to effect a diversion. "How about your carryings-on with the tortoise-shell puss up at the stables, eh?"

The moment he had said it every one realized the blunder.

"One does not usually discuss these matters in public," said Tobermory frigidly. "From a slight observation of your ways since you've been in this house I should imagine you'd find it inconvenient if I were to shift the conversation to your own little affairs."

The panic which ensued was not confined to the Major.

"Would you like to go and see if cook has got your dinner ready?" suggested Lady Blemley hurriedly, affecting to ignore the fact that it wanted at least two hours to Tobermory's dinner-time.

"Thanks," said Tobermory, "not quite so soon after my tea. I don't want to die of indigestion."

"Cats have nine lives, you know," said Sir Wilfred heartily.

"Possibly," answered Tobermory; "but only one liver."

"Adelaide!" said Mrs. Cornett, "do you mean to

encourage that cat to go out and gossip about us in the servants' hall?"

The panic had indeed become general. A narrow ornamental balustrade ran in front of most of the bedroom windows at the Towers, and it was recalled with dismay that this had formed a favourite promenade for Tobermory at all hours, whence he could watch the pigeons—and heaven knew what else besides. If he intended to become reminiscent in his present outspoken strain the effect would be something more than disconcerting. Mrs. Cornett, who spent much time at her toilet table, and whose complexion was reputed to be of a nomadic though punctual disposition, looked as ill at ease as the Major. Miss Scrawen, who wrote fiercely sensuous poetry and led a blameless life, merely displayed irritation; if you are methodical and virtuous in private you don't necessarily want everyone to know it. Bertie van Tahn, who was so depraved at 17 that he had long ago given up trying to be any worse, turned a dull shade of gardenia white, but he did not commit the error of dashing out of the room like Odo Finsberry, a young gentleman who was understood to be reading for the Church and who was possibly disturbed at the thought of scandals he might hear concerning other people. Clovis had the presence of mind to maintain a composed exterior; privately he was calculating how long it would take to procure a box of fancy mice through the agency of the

                        The Very Best Classic Short Stories

Exchange and Mart as a species of hush-money.

Even in a delicate situation like the present, Agnes Resker could not endure to remain long in the background.

"Why did I ever come down here?" she asked dramatically.

Tobermory immediately accepted the opening.

"Judging by what you said to Mrs. Cornett on the croquet-lawn yesterday, you were out of food. You described the Blemleys as the dullest people to stay with that you knew, but said they were clever enough to employ a first-rate cook; otherwise they'd find it difficult to get any one to come down a second time."

"There's not a word of truth in it! I appeal to Mrs. Cornett—" exclaimed the discomfited Agnes.

"Mrs. Cornett repeated your remark afterwards to Bertie van Tahn," continued Tobermory, "and said, 'That woman is a regular Hunger Marcher; she'd go anywhere for four square meals a day,' and Bertie van Tahn said—"

At this point the chronicle mercifully ceased. Tobermory had caught a glimpse of the big yellow tom from the Rectory working his way through the shrubbery towards the stable wing. In a flash he had vanished through the open French window.

With the disappearance of his too brilliant pupil Cornelius Appin found himself beset by a hurricane of bitter upbraiding, anxious inquiry, and frightened entreaty. The responsibility for the situation lay with him, and he must prevent matters from becoming worse. Could Tobermory impart his dangerous gift to other cats? was the first question he had to answer. It was possible, he replied, that he might have initiated his intimate friend the stable puss into his new accomplishment, but it was unlikely that his teaching could have taken a wider range as yet.

"Then," said Mrs. Cornett, "Tobermory may be a valuable cat and a great pet; but I'm sure you'll agree, Adelaide, that both he and the stable cat must be done away with without delay."

"You don't suppose I've enjoyed the last quarter of an hour, do you?" said Lady Blemley bitterly. "My husband and I are very fond of Tobermory—at least, we were before this horrible accomplishment was infused into him; but now, of course, the only thing is to have him destroyed as soon as possible."

"We can put some strychnine in the scraps he always gets at dinner-time," said Sir Wilfred, "and I will go and drown the stable cat myself. The coachman will be very sore at losing his pet, but I'll say a very catching form of mange has broken out in both cats and we're afraid of it spreading to the kennels."

"But my great discovery!" expostulated Mr. Appin; "after all my years of research and experiment—"

"You can go and experiment on the short-horns at the farm, who are under proper control," said Mrs. Cornett, "or the elephants at the Zoological Gardens. They're said to be highly intelligent, and they have this recommendation, that they don't come creeping about our bedrooms and under chairs, and so forth."

An archangel ecstatically proclaiming the Millennium, and then finding that it clashed unpardonably with Henley and would have to be indefinitely postponed, could hardly have felt more crestfallen than Cornelius Appin at the reception of his wonderful achievement. Public opinion, however, was against him—in fact, had the general voice been consulted on the subject it is probable that a strong minority vote would have been in favour of including him in the strychnine diet.

Defective train arrangements and a nervous desire to see matters brought to a finish prevented an immediate dispersal of the party, but dinner that evening was not a social success. Sir Wilfred had had rather a trying time with the stable cat and subsequently with the coach-man. Agnes Resker ostentatiously limited her repast to a morsel of dry toast, which she bit as though it were a personal enemy; while Mavis Pellington maintained a vindictive silence throughout the meal. Lady Blemley kept up a flow of what she hoped was conversation, but her attention was fixed on the doorway. A plateful of carefully dosed fish scraps was in readiness on the sideboard, but the sweets and savoury and dessert went their way, and no Tobermory appeared in the din-ing-room or kitchen.

The sepulchral dinner was cheerful compared with the subsequent vigil in the smoking-room. Eating and drinking had at least supplied a distraction and cloak to the prevailing embarrassment. Bridge was out of the question in the general tension of nerves and tempers, and after Odo Finsberry had given a lugubrious ren-dering of 'Melisande in the Wood' to a frigid audience, music was tacitly avoided. At eleven the servants went to bed, announcing that the small window in the pantry had been left open as usual for Tobermory's private use. The guests read steadily through the current batch of magazines, and fell back gradually on the "Badminton Library" and bound volumes of Punch. Lady Blemley made periodic visits to the pantry, returning each time with an expression of listless depression which fore-stalled questioning.

    The Very Best Classic Short Stories

At two o'clock Clovis broke the dominating silence.

"He won't turn up tonight. He's probably in the local newspaper office at the present moment, dictating the first installment of his reminiscences. Lady What's-her-name's book won't be in it. It will be the event of the day."

Having made this contribution to the general cheerfulness, Clovis went to bed. At long intervals the various members of the house-party followed his example.

The servants taking round the early tea made a uniform announcement in reply to a uniform question. Tobermory had not returned.

Breakfast was, if anything, a more unpleasant function than dinner had been, but before its conclusion the situation was relieved. Tobermory's corpse was brought in from the shrubbery, where a gardener had just discovered it. From the bites on his throat and the yellow fur which coated his claws it was evident that he had fallen in unequal combat with the big Tom from the Rectory.

By midday most of the guests had quitted the Towers, and after lunch Lady Blemley had sufficiently recovered her spirits to write an extremely nasty letter to the Rectory about the loss of her valuable pet.

Tobermory had been Appin's one successful pupil, and he was destined to have no successor. A few weeks later an elephant in the Dresden Zoological Garden, which had shown no previous signs of irritability, broke loose and killed an Englishman who had apparently been teasing it. The victim's name was variously reported in the papers as Oppin and Eppelin, but his front name was faithfully rendered Cornelius.

"If he was trying German irregular verbs on the poor beast," said Clovis, "he deserved all he got."

UP IN THE GALLERY

Franz Kafka

(Translation by Ian Johnston)

If some frail tubercular lady circus rider were to be
driven in circles around and around the arena for
months and months without interruption in front
of a tireless public on a swaying horse by a merciless
whip-wielding master of ceremonies, spinning on the
horse, throwing kisses and swaying at the waist, and
if this performance, amid the incessant roar of the
orchestra and the ventilators, were to continue into the
ever-expanding, gray future, accompanied by applause,
which died down and then swelled up again, from
hands which were really steam hammers, perhaps then
a young visitor to the gallery might rush down the long
stair case through all the levels, burst into the ring,
and cry "Halt!" through the fanfares of the constantly
adjusting orchestra.

But since things are not like that—since a beautiful
woman, in white and red, flies in through curtains
which proud men in livery open in front of her, since
the director, devotedly seeking her eyes, breathes in her
direction, behaving like an animal, and, as a precaution,
lifts her up on the dapple-gray horse, as if she were his
granddaughter, the one he loved more than anything
else, as she starts a dangerous journey, but he cannot
decide to give the signal with his whip and finally,

controlling himself, gives it a crack, runs right beside the horse with his mouth open, follows the rider's leaps with a sharp gaze, hardly capable of comprehending her skill, tries to warn her by calling out in English, furiously castigating the grooms holding hoops, telling them to pay the most scrupulous attention, and begs the orchestra, with upraised arms, to be quiet before the great jump, finally lifts the small woman down from the trembling horse, kisses her on both cheeks, considers no public tribute adequate, while she herself, leaning on him, high on the tips of her toes, with dust swirling around her, arms outstretched and head thrown back, wants to share her luck with the entire circus—since this is how things are, the visitor to the gallery puts his face on the railing and, sinking into the final march as if into a difficult dream, weeps, without realizing it.

    The Very Best Classic Short Stories

WAKEFIELD

Nathaniel Hawthorne

In some old magazine or newspaper I recollect a story, told as truth, of a man—let us call him Wakefield—who absented himself for a long time from his wife. The fact, thus abstractedly stated, is not very uncommon, nor, without a proper distinction of circumstances, to be condemned either as naughty or nonsensical. Howbeit, this, though far from the most aggravated, is perhaps the strangest instance on record of marital delinquency, and, moreover, as remarkable a freak as may be found in the whole list of human oddities. The wedded couple lived in London. The man, under pretence of going a journey, took lodgings in the next street to his own house, and there, unheard of by his wife or friends and without the shadow of a reason for such self-banishment, dwelt upward of twenty years. During that period he beheld his home every day, and frequently the forlorn Mrs. Wakefield. And after so great a gap in his matrimonial felicity—when his death was reckoned certain, his estate settled, his name dismissed from memory and his wife long, long ago resigned to her autumnal widowhood—he entered the door one evening quietly as from a day's absence, and became a loving spouse till death.

This outline is all that I remember. But the incident, though of the purest originality, unexampled, and probably never to be repeated, is one, I think, which appeals to the general sympathies of mankind. We know, each for himself, that none of us would perpetrate such a folly, yet feel as if some other might. To my own contemplations, at least, it has often recurred, always exciting wonder, but with a sense that the story must be true and a conception of its hero's character. Whenever any subject so forcibly affects the mind, time is well spent in thinking of it. If the reader choose, let him do his own meditation; or if he prefer to ramble with me through the twenty years of Wakefield's vagary, I bid him welcome, trusting that there will be a pervading spirit and a moral, even should we fail to find them, done up neatly and condensed into the final sentence. Thought has always its efficacy and every striking incident its moral.

What sort of a man was Wakefield? We are free to shape out our own idea and call it by his name. He was now in the meridian of life; his matrimonial affections, never violent, were sobered into a calm, habitual sentiment; of all husbands, he was likely to be the most constant, because a certain sluggishness would keep his heart at rest wherever it might be placed. He was intellectual, but not actively so; his mind occupied itself in long and lazy musings that tended to no purpose or had not vigor to attain it; his thoughts were seldom so energetic as to seize hold of words. Imagination, in the proper meaning of the term, made no part of

　　　　　　　　The Very Best Classic Short Stories

Wakefield's gifts. With a cold but not depraved nor wandering heart, and a mind never feverish with riotous thoughts nor perplexed with originality, who could have anticipated that our friend would entitle himself to a foremost place among the doers of eccentric deeds? Had his acquaintances been asked who was the man in London the surest to perform nothing to-day which should be remembered on the morrow, they would have thought of Wakefield. Only the wife of his bosom might have hesitated. She, without having analyzed his character, was partly aware of a quiet selfishness that had rusted into his inactive mind; of a peculiar sort of vanity, the most uneasy attribute about him; of a disposition to craft which had seldom produced more positive effects than the keeping of petty secrets hardly worth revealing; and, lastly, of what she called a little strangeness sometimes in the good man. This latter quality is indefinable, and perhaps non-existent.

Let us now imagine Wakefield bidding adieu to his wife. It is the dusk of an October evening. His equipment is a drab greatcoat, a hat covered with an oil-cloth, top-boots, an umbrella in one hand and a small portmanteau in the other. He has informed Mrs. Wakefield that he is to take the night-coach into the country. She would fain inquire the length of his journey, its object and the probable time of his return, but, indulgent to his harmless love of mystery, interrogates him only by

a look. He tells her not to expect him positively by the
return-coach nor to be alarmed should he tarry three
or four days, but, at all events, to look for him at supper
on Friday evening. Wakefield, himself, be it considered,
has no suspicion of what is before him. He holds out
his hand; she gives her own and meets his parting kiss
in the matter-of-course way of a ten years' matrimo-
ny, and forth goes the middle-aged Mr. Wakefield,
almost resolved to perplex his good lady by a whole
week's absence. After the door has closed behind him,
she perceives it thrust partly open and a vision of her
husband's face through the aperture, smiling on her
and gone in a moment. For the time this little incident
is dismissed without a thought, but long afterward,
when she has been more years a widow than a wife, that
smile recurs and flickers across all her reminiscences
of Wakefield's visage. In her many musings she sur-
rounds the original smile with a multitude of fantasies
which make it strange and awful; as, for instance, if she
imagines him in a coffin, that parting look is frozen on
his pale features; or if she dreams of him in heaven, still
his blessed spirit wears a quiet and crafty smile. Yet for
its sake, when all others have given him up for dead, she
sometimes doubts whether she is a widow.

But our business is with the husband. We must hurry
after him along the street ere he lose his individuality
and melt into the great mass of London life. It would

be vain searching for him there. Let us follow close at his heels, therefore, until, after several superfluous turns and doublings, we find him comfortably established by the fireside of a small apartment previously bespoken. He is in the next street to his own and at his journey's end. He can scarcely trust his good-fortune in having got thither unperceived, recollecting that at one time he was delayed by the throng in the very focus of a lighted lantern, and again there were footsteps that seemed to tread behind his own, distinct from the multitudinous tramp around him, and anon he heard a voice shouting afar and fancied that it called his name. Doubtless a dozen busybodies had been watching him and told his wife the whole affair.

Poor Wakefield! little knowest thou thine own insignificance in this great world. No mortal eye but mine has traced thee. Go quietly to thy bed, foolish man, and on the morrow, if thou wilt be wise, get thee home to good Mrs. Wakefield and tell her the truth. Remove not thyself even for a little week from thy place in her chaste bosom. Were she for a single moment to deem thee dead or lost or lastingly divided from her, thou wouldst be woefully conscious of a change in thy true wife for ever after. It is perilous to make a chasm in human affections—not that they gape so long and wide, but so quickly close again.

Almost repenting of his frolic, or whatever it may be termed, Wakefield lies down betimes, and, starting from his first nap, spreads forth his arms into the wide and solitary waste of the unaccustomed bed, "No," thinks he, gathering the bedclothes about him; "I will not sleep alone another night." In the morning he rises earlier than usual and sets himself to consider what he really means to do. Such are his loose and rambling modes of thought that he has taken this very singular step with the consciousness of a purpose, indeed, but without being able to define it sufficiently for his own contemplation. The vagueness of the project and the convulsive effort with which he plunges into the execution of it are equally characteristic of a feeble-minded man. Wakefield sifts his ideas, however, as minutely as he may, and finds himself curious to know the progress of matters at home—how his exemplary wife will endure her widowhood of a week, and, briefly, how the little sphere of creatures and circumstances in which he was a central object will be affected by his removal. A morbid vanity, therefore, lies nearest the bottom of the affair. But how is he to attain his ends? Not, certainly, by keeping close in this comfortable lodging, where, though he slept and awoke in the next street to his home, he is as effectually abroad as if the stage-coach had been whirling him away all night. Yet should he reappear, the whole project is knocked in the head. His

 The Very Best Classic Short Stories

poor brains being hopelessly puzzled with this dilemma, he at length ventures out, partly resolving to cross the head of the street and send one hasty glance toward his forsaken domicile. Habit—for he is a man of habits—takes him by the hand and guides him, wholly unaware, to his own door, where, just at the critical moment, he is aroused by the scraping of his foot upon the step.—Wakefield, whither are you going?

At that instant his fate was turning on the pivot. Little dreaming of the doom to which his first backward step devotes him, he hurries away, breathless with agitation hitherto unfelt, and hardly dares turn his head at the distant corner. Can it be that nobody caught sight of him? Will not the whole household—the decent Mrs. Wakefield, the smart maid-servant and the dirty little footboy—raise a hue-and-cry through London streets in pursuit of their fugitive lord and master? Wonderful escape! He gathers courage to pause and look homeward, but is perplexed with a sense of change about the familiar edifice such as affects us all when, after a separation of months or years, we again see some hill or lake or work of art with which we were friends of old. In ordinary cases this indescribable impression is caused by the comparison and contrast between our imperfect reminiscences and the reality. In Wakefield the magic of a single night has wrought a similar transformation, because in that brief period a great moral change has been effected. But this is a secret from himself. Before leaving the spot he catches a far and momentary glimpse of his wife passing athwart the front window with her face turned toward the head of the street. The crafty nincompoop takes to his heels, scared with the idea that among a thousand such atoms of mortality her eye must have detected him. Right glad is his heart, though his brain be somewhat dizzy, when he finds himself by the coal-fire of his lodgings.

So much for the commencement of this long whim-wham. After the initial conception and the stirring up of the man's sluggish temperament to put it in practice, the whole matter evolves itself in a natural train. We may suppose him, as the result of deep deliberation, buying a new wig of reddish hair and selecting sundry garments, in a fashion unlike his customary suit of brown, from a Jew's old-clothes bag. It is accomplished: Wakefield is another man. The new system being now established, a retrograde movement to the old would be almost as difficult as the step that placed him in his unparalleled position. Furthermore, he is rendered obstinate by a sulkiness occasionally incident to his temper and brought on at present by the inadequate sensation which he conceives to have been produced in the bosom of Mrs. Wakefield. He will not go back until she be frightened half to death. Well, twice or thrice has she passed before his sight, each time with a heavier step,

   The Very Best Classic Short Stories

a paler cheek and more anxious brow, and in the third week of his non-appearance he detects a portent of evil entering the house in the guise of an apothecary. Next day the knocker is muffled. Toward nightfall comes the chariot of a physician and deposits its big-wigged and solemn burden at Wakefield's door, whence after a quarter of an hour's visit he emerges, perchance the herald of a funeral. Dear woman! will she die?

By this time Wakefield is excited to something like energy of feeling, but still lingers away from his wife's bedside, pleading with his conscience that she must not be disturbed at such a juncture. If aught else restrains him, he does not know it. In the course of a few weeks she gradually recovers. The crisis is over; her heart is sad, perhaps, but quiet, and, let him return soon or late, it will never be feverish for him again. Such ideas glimmer through the mist of Wakefield's mind and render him indistinctly conscious that an almost impassable gulf divides his hired apartment from his former home. "It is but in the next street," he sometimes says. Fool! it is in another world. Hitherto he has put off' his return from one particular day to another; henceforward he leaves the precise time undetermined—not to-morrow; probably next week; pretty soon. Poor man! The dead have nearly as much chance of revisiting their earthly homes as the self-banished Wakefield.

Would that I had a folio to write, instead of an article of a dozen pages! Then might I exemplify how an influence beyond our control lays its strong hand on every deed which we do and weaves its consequences into an iron tissue of necessity.

Wakefield is spellbound. We must leave him for ten years or so to haunt around his house without once crossing the threshold, and to be faithful to his wife with all the affection of which his heart is capable, while he is slowly fading out of hers. Long since, it must be remarked, he has lost the perception of singularity in his conduct.

Now for a scene. Amid the throng of a London street we distinguish a man, now waxing elderly, with few characteristics to attract careless observers, yet bearing in his whole aspect the handwriting of no common fate for such as have the skill to read it. He is meagre; his low and narrow forehead is deeply wrinkled; his eyes, small and lustreless, sometimes wander apprehensively about him, but oftener seem to look inward. He bends his head and moves with an indescribable obliquity of gait, as if unwilling to display his full front to the world. Watch him long enough to see what we have described, and you will allow that circumstances—which often produce remarkable men from Nature's ordinary hand-iwork—have produced one such here. Next, leaving him to sidle along the footwalk, cast your eyes in the opposite direction, where a portly female considerably in the wane of life, with a prayer-book in her hand, is proceeding to yonder church. She has the placid mien of settled widowhood. Her regrets have either died away or have become so essential to her heart that they would be poorly exchanged for joy. Just as the lean man and well-conditioned woman are passing a slight obstruction occurs and brings these two figures directly in contact. Their hands touch; the pressure of the crowd forces her bosom against his shoulder; they stand face to face, staring into each other's eyes. After a ten years' separation thus Wakefield meets his wife. The throng eddies away and carries them asunder. The sober widow, resuming her former pace, proceeds to church, but pauses in the portal and throws a perplexed glance along the street. She passes in, however, opening her prayer-book as she goes.

And the man? With so wild a face that busy and selfish London stands to gaze after him he hurries to his lodgings, bolts the door and throws himself upon the bed. The latent feelings of years break out; his feeble mind acquires a brief energy from their strength; all the miserable strangeness of his life is revealed to him at a glance, and he cries out passionately, "Wakefield, Wakefield! You are mad!" Perhaps he was so. The singularity of his situation must have so moulded him to itself that, considered in regard to his fellow-creatures and the business of life, he could not be said to possess his right mind. He had contrived—or, rather, he had happened—to dissever himself from the world, to vanish, to give up his place and privileges with living men without being admitted among the dead. The life of a hermit is nowise parallel to his. He was in the bustle of the city as of old, but the crowd swept by and saw him not; he was, we may figuratively say, always beside his wife and at his hearth, yet must never feel the warmth of the one nor the affection of the other. It was Wakefield's unprecedented fate to retain his original share of human sympathies and to be still involved in human interests, while he had lost his reciprocal influence on them. It would be a most curious speculation to trace out the effect of such circumstances on his heart and intellect separately and in unison. Yet, changed as he was, he would seldom be conscious of it, but deem himself the same man as ever; glimpses of the truth, indeed, would come, but only for the moment, and still he would keep saying, "I shall soon go back," nor reflect that he had been saying so for twenty years.

I conceive, also, that these twenty years would appear in the retrospect scarcely longer than the week to which Wakefield had at first limited his absence. He would look on the affair as no more than an interlude in the main business of his life. When, after a little while more, he should deem it time to re-enter his parlor, his wife would clap her hands for joy on beholding the middle-aged Mr. Wakefield. Alas, what a mistake! Would Time but await the close of our favorite follies, we should be young men—all of us—and till Dooms-day.

One evening, in the twentieth year since he vanished, Wakefield is taking his customary walk toward the dwelling which he still calls his own. It is a gusty night of autumn, with frequent showers that patter down upon the pavement and are gone before a man can put up his umbrella. Pausing near the house, Wakefield discerns through the parlor-windows of the second floor the red glow and the glimmer and fitful flash of a comfortable fire. On the ceiling appears a grotesque shadow of good Mrs. Wakefield. The cap, the nose and chin and the broad waist form an admirable caricature, which dances, moreover, with the up-flickering and down-sinking blaze almost too merrily for the shade of an elderly widow. At this instant a shower chances to fall, and is driven by the unmannerly gust full into Wakefield's face and bosom. He is quite penetrated with its autumnal chill. Shall he stand wet and shivering here, when his own hearth has a good fire to warm him and his own wife will run to fetch the gray coat and small-clothes which doubtless she has kept carefully in the closet of their bedchamber? No; Wakefield is no

such fool. He ascends the steps—heavily, for twenty
years have stiffened his legs since he came down, but he
knows it not.—Stay, Wakefield! Would you go to the
sole home that is left you? Then step into your grave.—
The door opens. As he passes in we have a parting
glimpse of his visage, and recognize the crafty smile
which was the precursor of the little joke that he has
ever since been playing off at his wife's expense. How
unmercifully has he quizzed the poor woman! Well, a
good night's rest to Wakefield!

This happy event—supposing it to be such—could
only have occurred at an unpremeditated moment.
We will not follow our friend across the threshold. He
has left us much food for thought, a portion of which
shall lend its wisdom to a moral and be shaped into a
figure. Amid the seeming confusion of our mysterious
world individuals are so nicely adjusted to a system, and
systems to one another and to a whole, that by stepping
aside for a moment a man exposes himself to a fearful
risk of losing his place for ever. Like Wakefield, he may
become, as it were, the outcast of the universe.

THE
QUINCE TREE

Saki

"I've just been to see old Betsy Mullen," announced Vera to her aunt, Mrs. Bebberly Cumble; "she seems in rather a bad way about her rent. She owes about fifteen weeks of it, and says she doesn't know where any of it is to come from."

"Betsy Mullen always is in difficulties with her rent, and the more people help her with it the less she troubles about it," said the aunt. "I certainly am not going to assist her any more. The fact is, she will have to go into a smaller and cheaper cottage; there are several to be had at the other end of the village for half the rent that she is paying, or supposed to be paying, now. I told her a year ago that she ought to move."

"But she wouldn't get such a nice garden anywhere else," protested Vera, "and there's such a jolly quince tree in the corner. I don't suppose there's another quince tree in the whole parish. And she never makes any quince jam; I think to have a quince tree and not to make quince jam shows such strength of character. Oh, she can't possibly move away from that garden."

"When one is sixteen," said Mrs. Bebberly Cumble severely, "one talks of things being impossible which are merely uncongenial. It is not only possible but it is desirable that Betsy Mullen should move into smaller quarters; she has scarcely enough furniture to fill that big cottage."

"As far as value goes," said Vera after a short pause, "there is more in Betsy's cottage than in any other house for miles round."

"Nonsense," said the aunt; "she parted with whatever old china ware she had long ago."

"I'm not talking about anything that belongs to Betsy herself," said Vera darkly; "but, of course, you don't know what I know, and I don't suppose I ought to tell you."

"You must tell me at once," exclaimed the aunt, her senses leaping into alertness like those of a terrier suddenly exchanging a bored drowsiness for the lively anticipation of an immediate rat hunt.

"I'm perfectly certain that I oughtn't to tell you anything about it," said Vera, "but, then, I often do things that I oughtn't to do."

"I should be the last person to suggest that you should do anything that you ought not to do to — " began Mrs. Bebberly Cumble impressively.

"And I am always swayed by the last person who

     The Very Best Classic Short Stories

speaks to me," admitted Vera, "so I'll do what I ought not to do and tell you."

Mrs. Bebberley Cumble thrust a very pardonable sense of exasperation into the background of her mind and demanded impatiently:

"What is there in Betsy Mullen's cottage that you are making such a fuss about?"

"It's hardly fair to say that I've made a fuss about it," said Vera; "this is the first time I've mentioned the matter, but there's been no end of trouble and mystery and newspaper speculation about it. It's rather amusing to think of the columns of conjecture in the Press and the police and detectives hunting about everywhere at home and abroad, and all the while that innocent-looking little cottage has held the secret."

"You don't mean to say it's the Louvre picture, La Something or other, the woman with the smile, that disappeared about two years ago?" exclaimed the aunt with rising excitement.

"Oh no, not that," said Vera, "but something quite as important and just as mysterious — if anything, rather more scandalous."

"Not the Dublin — ?"

Vera nodded.

"The whole jolly lot of them."

"In Betsy's cottage? Incredible!"

"Of course Betsy hasn't an idea as to what they are," said Vera; "she just knows that they are something valuable and that she must keep quiet about them. I found out quite by accident what they were and how they came to be there. You see, the people who had them were at their wits' end to know where to stow them away for safe keeping, and some one who was motoring through the village was struck by the snug loneliness of the cottage and thought it would be just the thing. Mrs. Lamper arranged the matter with Betsy and smuggled the things in."

"Mrs. Lamper?"

"Yes; she does a lot of district visiting, you know."

"I am quite aware that she takes soup and flannel and improving literature to the poorer cottagers," said Mrs. Bebberly Cumble, "but that is hardly the same sort of thing as disposing of stolen goods, and she must have known something about their history; anyone who reads the papers, even casually, must have been aware of the theft, and I should think the things were not hard to recognise. Mrs. Lamper has always had the reputation of being a very conscientious woman."

"Of course she was screening some one else," said Vera. "A remarkable feature of the affair is the extraordinary number of quite respectable people who have involved themselves in its meshes by trying to shield others. You would be really astonished if you knew some of the names of the individuals mixed up in it, and I don't suppose a tithe of them know who the original culprits were; and now I've got you entangled in the mess by letting you into the secret of the cottage."

"You most certainly have not entangled me," said Mrs. Bebberly Cumble indignantly. "I have no intention of shielding anybody. The police must know about it at once; a theft is a theft, whoever is involved. If respectable people choose to turn themselves into receivers and disposers of stolen goods, well, they've ceased to be respectable, that's all. I shall telephone immediately — "

"Oh, aunt," said Vera reproachfully, "it would break the poor Canon's heart if Cuthbert were to be involved in a scandal of this sort. You know it would."

"Cuthbert involved! How can you say such things when you know how much we all think of him?"

"Of course I know you think a lot of him, and that

he's engaged to marry Beatrice, and that it will be a frightfully good match, and that he's your ideal of what a son-in-law ought to be. All the same, it was Cuthbert's idea to stow the things away in the cottage, and it was his motor that brought them. He was only doing it to help his friend Pegginson, you know — the Quaker man, who is always agitating for a smaller Navy. I forget how he got involved in it. I warned you that there were lots of quite respectable people mixed up in it, didn't I? That's what I meant when I said it would be impossible for old Betsy to leave the cottage; the things take up a good bit of room, and she couldn't go carrying them about with her other goods and chattels without attracting notice. Of course if she were to fall ill and die it would be equally unfortunate. Her mother lived to be over ninety, she tells me, so with due care and an absence of worry she ought to last for another dozen years at least. By that time perhaps some other arrangements will have been made for disposing of the wretched things."

"I shall speak to Cuthbert about it — after the wedding," said Mrs. Bebberly Cumble.

"The wedding isn't till next year," said Vera, in recounting the story to her best girl friend, "and meanwhile old Betsy is living rent free, with soup twice a week and my aunt's doctor to see her whenever she has a finger ache."

 The Very Best Classic Short Stories

"But how on earth did you get to know about it all?" asked her friend, in admiring wonder.

"It was a mystery — " said Vera.

"Of course it was a mystery, a mystery that baffled everybody. What beats me is how you found out — "

"Oh, about the jewels? I invented that part," explained Vera; "I mean the mystery was where old Betsy's arrears of rent were to come from; and she would have hated leaving that jolly quince tree."